THE
BROWN MOUSE
BOOK

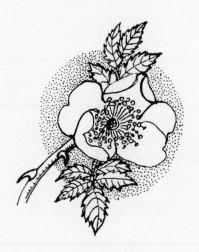

BOOKS BY
ALISON UTTLEY

THE
BROWN MOUSE
BOOK

Magical Tales of Two Little Mice

stories by
ALISON UTTLEY

pictures by
Katherine Wigglesworth

HEINEMANN : LONDON

William Heinemann Ltd.
15 Queen Street, Mayfair, London WIX 8BE
LONDON   MELBOURNE   TORONTO
JOHANNESBURG   AUCKLAND

First published in this edition 1971
Text © Alison Uttley 1971
Illustrations © Katherine Wigglesworth 1971

313185

Filmset and printed Offset Litho by
Cox & Wyman Ltd.
London, Fakenham and Reading

CONTENTS

Snug and Serena meet a Queen

Down the lane, sheltered by a wild rose bush, is a little house, hidden in the bank. It is so small you would not notice it unless you stooped and lifted the ferns and grasses, and moved away the curving rose sprays. You might hear the humming and singing and soft laughter if you stood 'as still as a mouse'.

The woodland animals know this place very well. They call it the 'Rose and Crown', and here they come for their tastes of cowslip wine and dandelion tea.

Over the door hangs the wooden sign, with a picture of a tiny rose and a crown. You might easily mistake it for an autumn leaf dangling from a twig.

There is a porch of twisted rose briars, and in it, on fine days, sit little fieldmice.

They drink from acorn mugs and they smoke clay pipes packed with mouse-baccy, which is wild thyme.

The curls of blue smoke float up in the branches of the rose bush and make a sweet smell.

Behind the cosy kitchen and dainty parlour are three or four tiny bedrooms, and store rooms and cellars, down long winding passages which go deep into the bank. In the store rooms are heaps of wheat and barley, the gleanings of the cornfields, and acorns, beech-mast and cob-nuts.

One bedroom with a goose-feather bed and a peg for a best jacket belongs to little Snug. It is always untidy. The blue jacket is seldom on its peg.

Next to it is the bedroom of Serena, his sister. There is a white bed of hollywood, polished like ivory, and a peg for the Sunday frock of white silk, and a cupboard for Serena's treasures. It is a neat room with a rug of thistledown and a rocking-chair.

Snug and Serena play all day in the bank near their home. They hide in the long grasses, they run down the shady paths among violets and primroses,

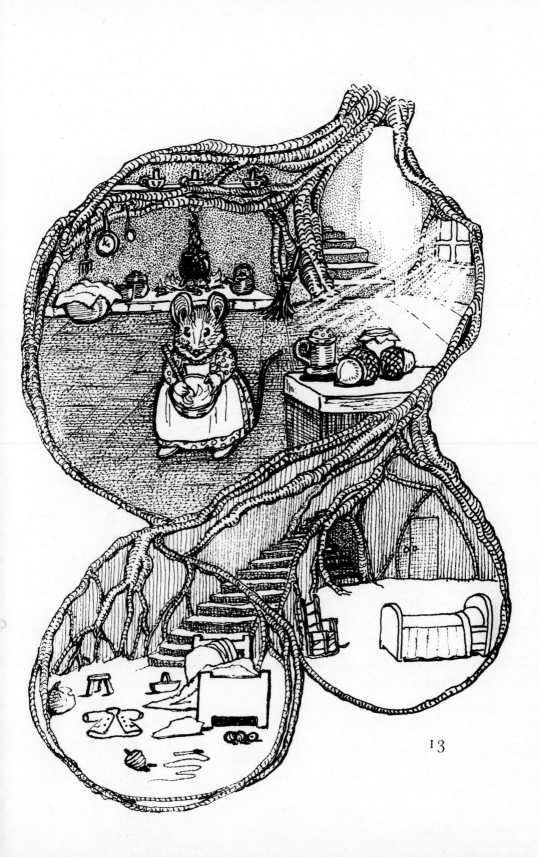

13

they suck honey from the cowslip's bell. When it rains they carry violet leaves for umbrellas, and they laugh at the raindrops.

One day Mrs Mouse was very busy. She was expecting a visitor, and there were cakes to be made, and corn to bake.

'Come along, Snug and Serena. Give me a hand,' she called from the doorway, and she rang a harebell to summon her children. They were up a tree, staring at the beetles and ladybirds down below in the lane. When they heard the tinkle of the bell they dropped to the ground.

Snug came running indoors, with his little blue jacket flapping. He tossed his red cap to the mice in the porch. Serena came tumbling after in her yellow skirt.

'Who's coming, mother?' they panted.

'I don't rightly know, childer,' replied Mrs Mouse who was frying the bacon rinds over a bright fire. 'I'm sure it's fine company for Robin the Postman brought a letter and only grand folk write on silver-birch bark with a gold crest on the back.'

Serena picked up the folded scrap of silver birch and Mrs Mouse read it again. 'xpect me to din.'

'It may be Mr Mole or Mr Frog,' said Serena.

'Or a Harvest Mouse,' said Snug.

'Or Tom Hedgehog,' said Serena.

'I think it's Royalty,' said Mrs Mouse, and she nodded her head and went back to her cooking.

'Fill the tea-kettle, Snug,' she cried, and Snug ran out to the stream with the tin kettle.

'Get me a mouse-lettuce, Serena,' she commanded, and Serena darted to the lane and picked the delicate sour leaves of the wood-sorrel.

'I want violet petals for a salad, Serena,' called her mother, 'and an egg for an omelette.'

Good little Serena picked the violets and then she climbed a hawthorn tree to a nest where a chaffinch sat.

'Have you a spare egg, please?' asked Serena. 'Mother's expecting company and she wants an egg.'

'Certainly not,' cried the indignant chaffinch, and she puffed out her feathers and pecked at Serena, till the little mouse nearly fell backwards in a fright.

Every nest she visited it was the same. Nobody

could spare an egg for Mrs Mouse's omelette. Serena had just decided that she must go to the farmyard and trundle an egg home, when the turtle-dove took pity on her.

'I'll leave an egg at your door,' said the dove, and the gentle bird flew down and laid an egg on the moss near the front door of the 'Rose and Crown'.

'Oh, thank you, thank you very much,' cried Mrs Mouse.

Serena stayed a moment to pick the sweet hawthorn leaves, which country children call 'bread-and-cheese'.

'Serena. Our Serena,' called a piping voice, and little Snug came to join her.

'I'm going to sit here and look out for the company.

Father says so. I'm the look-out mouse,' said he, proudly, and he stuck a little telescope of straw to his eye and peered all round.

'I wonder who it will be,' said Serena. 'I am glad we are going to have company.'

'They won't want you. Company sits all alone, very grand,' said Snug.

Serena ran home with her leaves and flowers, and Mrs Mouse chopped them and put them in the salad.

The bread-and-cheese went in one walnut shell, may-buds and mouse-lettuce in another, primroses and violets in a third. Serena whisked the dove's egg ready for the omelette.

Mr Mouse came puffing up from the cellars carrying bottles, cobwebbed and dirty.

'Must get all ready,' said he. 'Honeymead's a likely drink.'

He rubbed the bottles clean on his green baize apron and set them on the floor to warm in the sunshine.

'Mester Mouse, who are you expecting of?' called Timothy Snout, one of the ancients in the porch. 'Is it King and Queen? If so I mun be off to tidy myself.'

'I think it's Royalty, Timothy Snout,' said William Mouse, drawing out the corks with a pop.

'Bring me a mug of dandelion, if you please, to drink their healths,' cried another mouse, Samuel Furze. He lived in the gorse bush, and he was always thirsty.

'Mester Mouse. Bring me a jug of that honey-mead,' called a third, old John Barleycorn.

Suddenly there was a shout from the hawthorn tree.

'Here they are! Here they are! Hundreds of 'em.' Snug slipped down, catching his trousers on a thorn and hanging there for a minute as he shouted 'hundreds and hundreds'.

Then the trousers split and he fell among the startled mice near the door of the 'Rose and Crown'.

'I've seen them,' said Snug, excitedly. 'There's a glass coach rolling over the field with a crowd flying round it. Hundreds of 'em. It's the littlest coach you ever saw. It's got a gold crown on the top, like our sign.'

'I can hear them, all singing and humming,' said Serena, her hand to her pointed furry ear.

'It's the Queen Bee,' cried Mrs Mouse. 'It must be the Queen Bee swarming. You childer brush your hair and wash your hands while I tidy myself.

18

Queens are very particular.'

Serena and Snug sleeked their fur with tiny teasel brushes, and washed their hands and faces in the little bowl on the table.

'William, put on your best jacket, and get ready to receive the Queen,' continued Mrs Mouse. 'All of you must bow and curtsey. Remember your manners.'

'The Queen Bee,' said Mr Mouse slowly, and he put down the tankards he was carrying and untied his apron, and brushed his whiskers and head. Then he slipped on his best ruby coat.

'Deary me! I hope she isn't going to be a nuisance and bring her swarm here. We've no room for a swarm of bees. No room at all. What will happen to the "Rose and Crown" if all that crowd comes in?

There'd be no room for us. They'll sting us and drive us away. Deary me.'

'Put some mugs of honeymead on the bank and maybe she won't come in,' advised Timothy Snout.

'Set some honey-cakes on the grass, and shut the door,' said Samuel Furze.

'Beat your drum and bang your fire-irons,' said old John Barleycorn.

But before anyone could prepare, the humming grew very near, and a dark cloud of bees hovered outside the inn. From her glass coach the Queen Bee looked out.

'Stop,' she commanded. 'Here is the famous "Rose and Crown". We will live here. It's a good inn with food and rooms ready.'

Mrs Mouse came forward with a low curtsey, and Mr Mouse gave a nervous bow. Snug and Serena bobbed.

'Good-day, Your Majesty,' said they.

'A swarm of bees in May
    Is worth a load of hay'
piped old Timothy Snout.

'Yes, we are a valuable swarm,' said the Queen proudly. 'We will honour you with our company. We will take the "Rose and Crown" – lock, stock and barrel, wine, mead and barley-brew.'

Mr Mouse turned pale. He carried out a bowl of honey wine and the Queen dipped her own silver cup into it. She drank and then threw away the little

cup. All the bees hovered about, drinking the honey wine from the bottles and glasses.

'Landlord,' said the Queen. 'We shall want the whole of your inn, and food and wine.'

'Please, your Majesty, I don't think it is big enough to hold all of you,' stammered poor Mr Mouse.

'Not big enough for my bees and you, but you must move out,' said the Queen, coldly, and she stepped from the coach and came towards the door with the great crowd buzzing behind her.

Little Serena kept close to her mother and Mrs Mouse stood with her back to the door ready to defend her home. Then young Snug came forward.

'Please Your Majesty,' said he, bowing, 'I knows of a beautiful palace, white as snow, sweet as honey, with lots of room in it, and a fine doorway, and a garden of flowers.'

Everyone stared at Snug.

'Where is this palace?' asked the Queen Bee.

'At the farmhouse,' said Snug, simply. 'It's a new hive all ready for a swarm of bees. There's a stream near, and a clover field. You'll be welcome as a load of hay there, Your Majesty.'

'A clover field! A new hive! To the farm we will go,' said the Queen, and she climbed into the coach. 'If ever you want some honeycomb, knock at the palace door and one of my workers will give you some.'

She waved her hand and the swarm rose high in

the air with the coach in the middle. With a loud humming they flew away, over the field to the farm and the new hive.

Mrs Mouse trembled with relief, and Mr Mouse wiped his face with his large red handkerchief.

'Well done, Snug! You've saved the "Rose and Crown",' said he. 'I thought we should have to go.'

'How did you know about the hive?' asked Mrs Mouse.

'Oh, I saw it one day, when I was exploring,' said Snug.

'Crowns of gold are all right, but I like humble folk in leather leggings and jackets and scarves, not crowns of gold,' said Mr Mouse.

Little Serena came running up. 'Here's the silver cup the Queen threw away,' she cried, holding a tiny cup like a flower.

'And here's a gold slipper she lost,' added Snug, and he picked up the slipper from the grass.

'We'll keep them safe in memory of Royalty's visit,' said Mrs Mouse, and she put them in Serena's cupboard among her treasures.

'Another visitor's a-coming up the lane,' called Timothy Snout. 'It's the Toad, creeping along, slow as a snail.'

Up the lane waddled a Toad, with striped waistcoat, and yellow buttons and buff breeches. He hobbled along; he stared at the sky; he looked at the grass; he drank from a stream – he certainly took his time.

'Good-day, Timothy. Good-day, Samuel. Good-day John Barleycorn,' he greeted the mice, and he rapped at the inn door with the knob of his stick.

'Anyone at home?' he asked.

'Oh, come in, Mr Toad,' cried Mrs Mouse, smoothing her apron.

'Come in, sir,' said Mr Mouse, throwing wide the door.

The Toad rubbed his damp feet on the doormat for a long time, and then he put his stick in the corner of the room. He sat down in the armchair Mr Mouse brought forward for him, and he looked round with a broad smile.

'Did you get my letter, Ma'am?' he asked.

'Was it yours?' cried Mrs Mouse. 'We thought it was Royalty, and Royalty has just been here.'

'Royalty didn't eat my dinner, I hope,' said the Toad.

'No. The Queen Bee had a sip of honey wine but no more,' said Mrs Mouse, firmly. 'No more, although she wanted a lot.'

'There was a gold crest on the letter,' said Mr Mouse.

'Oh that! Yes, it was a bit of sunshine I caught in my fishing-net,' explained Mr Toad, airily. 'I stuck it on the letter to smarten it up.'

'It made us all hurry, Mr Toad,' said Mrs Mouse, smiling. 'Now I'll make the omelette, sir.' She whipped up the egg again and added the herbs.

Two little mice came out to stare at the Toad. They liked his big face, his bright eyes and humped head. They liked his webbed feet and his creased coat and bulky pockets.

'Now you two children,' said Mr Toad. 'What shall it be? A lollipop? A story? A present?'

'Whatever you like, Mr Toad,' stammered Serena.

'A lollipop first,' said Snug.

The Toad put his hand in his deep pocket and brought out some striped sweets wrapped in a king-cup leaf. From another pocket he brought a paint-box rolled up in silvery water-leaves, and from yet another came a willow cricket bat about two inches long, and lastly he fished out a beautiful little fiddle, called a jig, which he used for dances.

'Oh, thank you. Thank you, Mr Toad,' cried the young mice, and they sat on the floor with the lolli-pops between them, while the smiling old Toad told

them a fairy story.

'Once upon a time,' he began in his croaking voice. 'Once upon a time, there lived in the depths of a deep, deep well, a Royal Toad.'

'Dinner's ready,' called Mrs Mouse.

She had set the table with her clean cloth, and put on it her best rose-bud china, and wooden spoons and blue mugs and green glasses.

'Dinner's ready, please sir,' announced Mrs Mouse again and she rang the little harebell.

'You must all join me,' said Mr Toad, looking up. 'I don't want to dine alone. Everyone must come.'

'You won't go home, will you, Mr Toad?' asked Serena, pulling her chair close to Mr Toad's.

'Have you a spare room, Mrs Mouse?' asked the Toad, glancing towards her.

'A beautiful room, with running water for washing your feet,' said Mrs Mouse, proudly. 'There's a feather bed and clean sheets.'

'Then I'll stay the night, Mrs Mouse,' said he. 'I wanted to visit the "Rose and Crown", and sample Mrs Mouse's cooking. Tomorrow I shall go on my way to my castle, but tonight I will stay with your pleasant company.'

After dinner the Toad told them another tale, and played his fiddle to the two little mice. Mrs Mouse fetched her knitting and Mr Mouse smoked his pipe.

When dusk fell and the first star appeared in the

sky, the Toad asked for his candle. They took him to the spare room where a trickle of water flowed, and he said good night.

'This is just my kind of bedroom,' said he, dipping his toes in the stream.

Snug and Serena could hear him singing as they lay in their own small beds and the words came floating down the underground passage.

'Oh, the Rose and the Crown,
With green leaves and brown.
In summer and spring
The turtle-doves sing,
At the Rose and the Crown.
It is fit for a King,
Is the Rose and the Crown.'

'Is he Royal?' whispered Serena.
'Is he a King?' asked Snug.

The Flower Show

This is the story of how Snug and Serena went to a
Flower Show. It was not a mouse flower show in the
hedge bank where the wild thyme grows, but a
grown-up show in a tent to which fieldmice are not
invited.

One day Snug and Serena were playing hide-
and-seek in a hollow piece of oak. It was a small,
curly branch, silvery with lichen, and inside was a
hole lined with moss, leading to a tiny room. It was
so narrow only two small mice could enter.

'This is a secret house where we can hide,' said
little Serena. 'We can come here and nobody will
ever find us.'

'Why, there's a cupboard in here,' cried Snug.
'Let's fill it with honey and then we can stay as long

as we like.'

Off they ran to the wild bees' honeycomb in a tree, and they broke off a scrap and carried it to the cupboard. They were just going out to find more when they heard footsteps coming down the lane. They knew it was a human coming along.

They stayed very still, but their oak branch was lifted up.

'This is just what I want for my flower decoration,' said a voice.

Snug and Serena clung to one another.

'Are you frightened, Serena?' whispered Snug.

'No,' laughed Serena. 'Are you?'

'Not at all,' said Snug, boldly. 'It's an adventure. Let's see what happens.'

The lady took the hollow piece of wood to her cottage in the village. When Snug heard the church bell he knew where he was.

They tumbled about in the hollow, but they never made a squeak even when a cat came sniffing round.

'Go away, Puss! Go away!' said Miss Smith sternly. 'Don't dare to touch my lovely tree.'

The branch was fixed in a bowl of water. Hart's-tongue ferns were planted by it, and some flowers, with a bunch of green grapes to hang down the side.

'Very nice indeed,' said the voices, and everybody admired the lichened tree.

'The little mossy hole is most attractive,' said someone and a finger was poked inside the hollow.

Snug and Serena drew back.

'Shall I bite it?' whispered Snug, but Serena nudged him to be quiet.

'Tomorrow morning I shall take this to the Flower Show and I am sure I shall get a prize,' said Miss Smith.

'Did you hear that?' asked Snug. 'A Flower Show. I always wanted to see a real Flower Show.'

'There will be lots to eat,' said Serena eagerly. 'I'm getting so hungry, Snug. I'm glad we have this honey in the cupboard.'

They had supper and then they slept soundly. At dawn a ray of sunshine came through the tiny mossy doorway and they opened their eyes.

'Where am I?' asked Serena, sleepily.

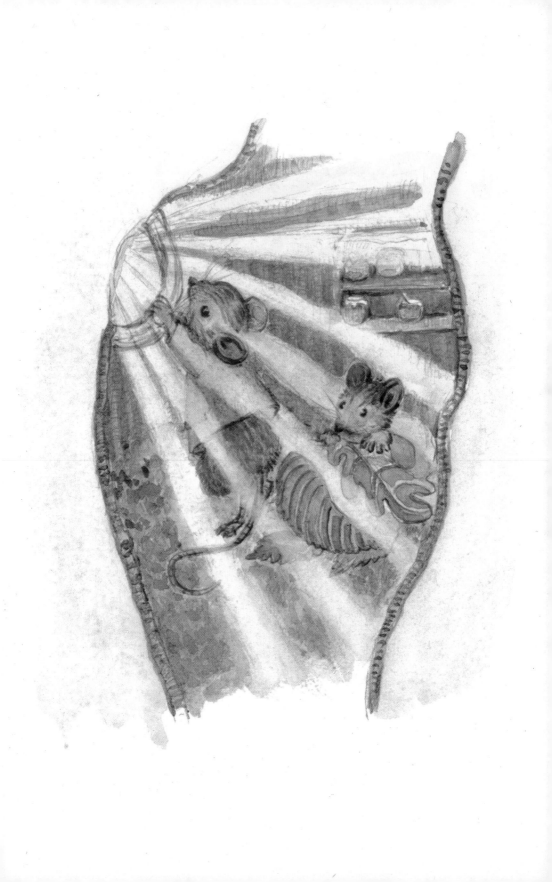

They both peeped timidly out but the cat was not there and the room was empty. They climbed down the branch, leapt over the water, and walked on the table. There were delicious morsels of food lying ready for them, bits of cheese, and some butter. The two wrinkled their noses with pleasure and ate a good breakfast. They were dancing about when they heard a sound, and they scurried back across the water into the hollow branch.

'Oh dear, I've lost a slipper,' murmured Serena, holding out her foot. 'It fell off when I ran so fast.'

Miss Smith came again to admire her bowl. She rearranged it, and then she carried it with its tree and fruit and flowers to the Flower Show. It was placed on a table among several other vases and bowls of flowers.

The tent was closed, and it was quiet. The little mice peered out.

They poked out their heads and their little paws, and then they stepped warily down the crooked silver oak.

They saw dishes of ripe plums, blue as night, and yellow pears and red apples. They cried out in surprise at the giant onions, tied in top-knots, and the long scarlet runners.

'Look! Look!' cried Serena, picking up her skirt and dancing on bare toes. They tasted the raspberries and plums, with little nibbles, and then they went across the tables to look at the strange flowers. There were roses like silk cushions upon which they could sit, and snapdragons which snapped their yellow mouths at them, and stocks which held parcels of perfume, and mignonette which carried little green purses full of mouse-money on their stalks.

Every flower nodded its head to the two little mice who fluttered like butterflies over the tables.

They came to the jam jars which the school children had filled with collections of wild flowers. There were harebells to ring, and willow-herb to climb like a ladder, and purple cushions of scabious which Mrs Mouse used for her pincushions, and tansy which she put in a pie, and scented meadow-sweet. 'All the flowers we know are here,' said Serena. 'Even wild thyme and marjoram.'

'Useful for soup,' said Snug, wisely.

'We'll give them all first prizes,' said Serena.

'First Prize' she wrote on a label in mouse-language.

The women of the village had made some little rock gardens in plates and dishes with sand for paths, and water, and a few plants growing among the rocks. When Snug and Serena found them, they ran along the paths, washed their faces in the pools and leapt from the rocks.

'Gardens for us,' laughed Serena. 'They must have guessed we were coming.'

They dragged some corn-stalks from a vase, and wove a little house from the straw, like a harvest mouse's nest. They put wheat ears at the top in a tassel. Then they placed the round straw house in one of the gardens, where it was like a fairy cot.

'Now let us make a basket from the grasses,' said Serena. 'Let's show them what we can do.'

36

They plaited a couple of grass baskets and filled them with flower heads and little berries.

They nibbled some rose petals to make lace mats and put them among the needlework.

'Humans do make big stitches,' observed Serena, looking at the white stitches in a cloth. 'They should see our mother's sewing.'

She began to sing:

> 'A mouse does the sewing
> With stitches so small
> You scarcely can see them
> At all, at all.
>
> A mouse does the mending,
> And no one can see,
> The patch or the darn,
> So wee, so wee.'

'Quiet!' hissed Snug. 'You'll wake the people.'

'Let us make our own bowls of flowers,' said Serena, hopping and skipping joyfully.

'Here's a flower-pot,' said Snug.

He held up a silver thimble which had been left on the table.

They filled the thimble with a bouquet of the

tiniest flowers. They put in miniature roses and florets of meadow-sweet, a daisy, sprigs of grasses, and bells, so that it was the prettiest little pot of flowers ever seen.

'I'm getting hungry,' said Serena. 'Find some food, Snug.'

They darted along the tables to the cookery exhibits. Cream cheeses, golden tarts, iced cakes, scones and pastry were arranged on plates ready for the judging.

'I do like a Flower Show like this,' said Snug, helping himself to the iced sponge cake. 'This is worth first prize.'

'All first prizes,' agreed Serena, dreamily, as she nibbled each cake.

There was a rumble of voices, the tent opened, and the judges entered.

'No time to get back,' muttered Snug. 'Run, Serena.' They scuttered down the table legs to the floor; they ran through the thick grass and escaped under the edge of the tent.

A voice cried out, 'Look! Look at these tiny vases! Flowers in a thimble! It's a fairy's work!'

Then another voice exclaimed. 'This straw house is remarkably well made. This is a gem of a garden, with little baskets of flowers.'

Somebody said, 'This flower arrangement with the lichened branch is clever, but what is sticking out of the mossy hole? A little red shoe? A yellow handkerchief?

'There!' cried Snug. 'You've gone and lost your other slipper!'

'And you've lost your hanky!' retorted Serena.

'Let us get away at once,' said Snug, so they did not hear the cries when the judges saw the cakes each with two little nibbles and two little bites.

'I know the way home,' said Snug. 'Follow me.'

They went along the invisible footpaths to the field.

They crossed the field and entered the lane and at last they saw the chimneys of the 'Rose and Crown', hidden under the rose tree. There was the dear mossy roof and the washing hanging out in the garden.

Mrs Mouse came running to meet them, crying, 'Oh, children, where have you been?'

'Serena and Snug,' scolded Mr Mouse, rushing

up from the cellar. 'You are very naughty indeed.'

'We've been to a Flower Show down by the church,' boasted Snug.

'We made baskets of flowers and a summer hut,' added Serena.

'And Serena lost her shoes, one in a house and one in the Flower Show,' said Snug.

'In a house! In a Flower Show!' Mrs Mouse nearly fainted.

Snug and Serena told their adventures, and the family listened astonished.

Down in the village the judges were puzzled.

'Mice have been tasting everything – a nibble here, a nibble there, just a bite,' said they.

'Fairies have been here to fill this thimble and to make these baskets of flowers,' said others.

'Is it mice or fairies?' asked a little girl.

'We really don't know,' confessed the judges. 'There was a tiny red slipper and a yellow hanky in that silvery tree, and Miss Smith found another red slipper on her kitchen floor. It is all very mysterious.'

'I think it was Snug and Serena,' said the little girl.

But everyone laughed, for how could she know?

Going to the Fair

One day Snug was trotting along a green track in the field when he saw a straw house under the hedge. It was a caravan made out of wheat-stalks, with a chimney on top, a door at the back, and a handle to pull it along.

At the door sat two harvest mice busily weaving little baskets of straw to hold grain.

Snug hid behind a dandelion, but the mice had seen him.

'I knew your red trousers, young Mousekin,' said Mr Harvest. 'I saw 'em once at the "Rose and Crown".'

'As red as corn poppies,' added Mrs Harvest.

'Can't help seeing you,' said Mr Harvest. 'But never mind our jokes. Just take a peep at the caravan.'

Snug ran into the straw house which held many little baskets fitted into one another.

'Do you live here?' he asked.

'No, we live in the cornfield,' said Mrs Harvest. 'We are basket-makers, on the way to the Fair.'

'The Fair?' echoed Snug. 'Where is it?'

'In the corner of the orchard,' said Mr Harvest. 'Everyone knows about it. You be off home and ask if they've forgotten the May Fair.'

As Snug ran he saw the yellow skirt of his sister Serena fluttering in the bushes like a brimstone butterfly.

'Hello, Serena,' he called. 'Have you heard there's

a Fair?'

Serena crept out of the gorse.

'A Fair?' she cried. 'Oh, let's go! I've never seen a Fair.'

When they got home there was a chatter and squeak in the 'Rose and Crown'. A gypsy hedgehog was there, with a basket of clothes-pegs made out of thorns like her own prickles.

'Yes, I'm going to the May Fair,' said she. 'It's in the orchard.'

She picked up her basket and then she stared at Snug.

'We shan't miss seeing you, in your red trousers,' said she. 'You're like a poppy in the corn.'

She laughed and away she went, singing.

'The rude prickly-bob,' pouted Snug. 'I'm not a poppy in the corn.'

'Now, everybody stop talking,' said Mrs Mouse, ringing her harebell for silence. 'We are going to the Fair and we must get ready at once.'

'I saw some basket-makers with a yellow caravan under the hedge. They told me,' cried Snug, eagerly.

'Be quiet and do as you're bid,' said Mrs Mouse. 'An unbiddable mouse stays at home. Snug and Serena wash yourselves.'

Mrs Mouse bustled around making lettuce and egg sandwiches. Serena and Snug washed their faces and brushed their fur. Mr Mouse struggled into his best coat.

The key he hid under a dandelion. Laughing, talking, the four set off down the narrow track at the side of the lane. They kept to the grass where they were safe. The path was worn by many small feet pattering there all day long and sometimes into the night.

They saw a butterfly fast in a spider's web and

little Snug unfastened the knots of silken rope and set her free.

'Thank you, Snug,' said the butterfly.

On they went, sipping from the honey-bags of the white dead-nettle, nibbling the sweet hawthorn leaves, biting sour wood-sorrel, blowing at dandelion clocks to find the time.

'Oh, there's the caravan with the basket-makers,' cried Snug, and over the grass trundled the little yellow house, with Mrs Harvest pushing and Mr Harvest pulling it.

'Going to the Fair?' called Mr Mouse, and the harvest mice nodded.

'A hard-working couple, those harvest mice,' said Mr Mouse. 'Good weavers and very knowledge-able about corn.'

Now they could hear the tinkling of flowery bells, the rattle of grasses, the music of a fiddle and a harp of silvery tone.

In the orchard among the flowers of spring, the

Fair was held. At first the mice walked about, looking at the stalls, admiring the display. There were piles of golden wheat and barley, of dried acorns and cobnuts, which had been stored all the winter and were put out for sale. Brown cakes and sugar sticks were heaped on broad sycamore leaves.

Little animals hurried to and fro, emptying their baskets for the customers to buy and the customers strolled about and met their friends and relations. Hedgehogs stood in one corner, buying clothes-pegs and teazle-brushes from the gypsy.

Mrs Mouse and Serena loitered by a ribbon stall,

and they bought some green-striped ribbon-grasses which had come from the garden beyond the wall.

They found a red pincushion and a walnut-shell box. There was a doll, too, made of poppy-petals and Serena bought it for a mouse-penny. Snug begged for a whip and top.

Suddenly, when all were enjoying themselves, a drum sounded, a rabbit's foot thumped the earth, and a trumpet squeaked. It was the alarm for DANGER!

Every little animal dropped to the ground and disappeared, either in the shelter of the wall, or down one of the narrow passages which go under-ground in fields and lanes and pastures to the safety caverns of the small animals of the wild. With them went Snug and Serena, running as fast as their little legs would carry them, Mrs Mouse panting behind and Mr Mouse following his family.

'What is it, father? A lion?' asked Snug, trembling with excitement.

'Only a hawk, my son,' said Mr Mouse, calmly. 'Always hide when a wind-hover appears. If you don't hide, then be still and it may not see you.'

Ribbons and laces fell to the ground, toys were scattered. The harvest mice had gone into their caravan, the hedgehogs rolled themselves in balls. The animals whispered as they watched the hawk's shadow pass over the ground. Then away flew the keen-eyed bird and the Fair went on.

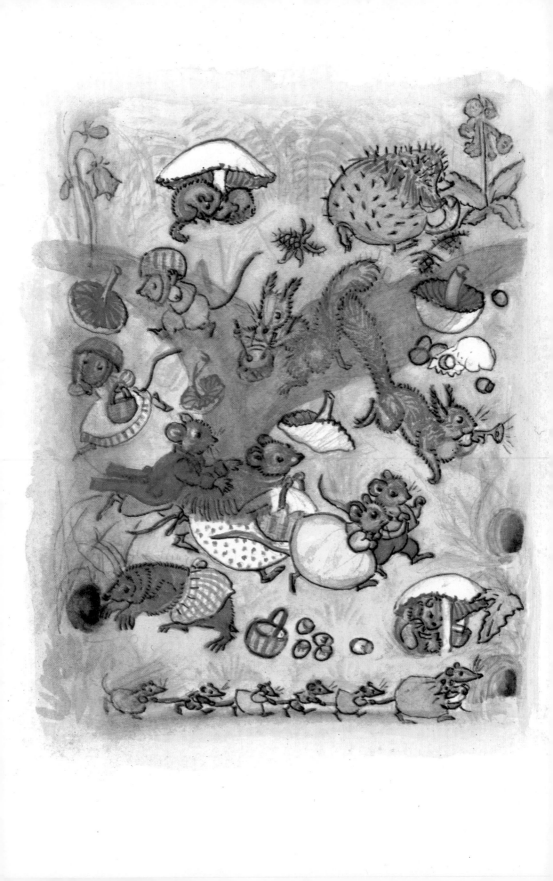

'Oh dear!' sighed Mrs Mouse. 'I can't abide hawks. They are like cats flying up there, with sharp eyes and fierce claws.'

'Why, there's Timothy Snout and Samuel Furze and John Barleycorn,' shouted Mr Mouse, hailing his old friends.

'I've brought my family to see the Fair,' he told them, and Mrs Mouse bobbed a curtsey and the three ancient mice bowed to her.

'Join us at dinner,' suggested Mrs Mouse. 'We have enough for everybody. Come and sit with us.'

So they sat on the sunny bank. John Barleycorn brought a few honey cakes from his pocket, and laid them on the grass, and Timothy added a round cheese his wife had made. Then Samuel put out a lardy-cake – and what a feast they had!

Snug and Serena dipped their toes in the stream and fished for minnows with rods made of green rushes. Tim Rabbit came up and played his flute for them to dance.

Little Tom Hedgehog showed Serena how to play darts, and Wat Hare tossed his cowslip ball into her lap for a present.

'Now we'll go and buy some fairings,' said Timothy Snout, and he took his leather purse from his pocket and counted his green pennies.

For Serena he bought a necklace of blue beads, made from the seeds of a rare flower in the garden.

Snug chose a humming-top which played a tune.

It had been carved from a nut by a champion carver.

Then Snug wandered off alone, exploring the big orchard. 'There's music somewhere,' he whispered to himself, and, indeed, a queer little air had been tinkling through the fairground.

Behind the bee-hive, hanging from the low bough of an apple-tree was a swing, and near it fat Pin Hedgehog, ragged and rough, played a mouth-organ.

'Can I have a swing?' asked Snug, holding out his penny, and the old scarecrow nodded.

'Be ye careful. Many a Mouse gets Missed,' said he.

Then away soared the swing, up towards the sky, down to the ground. The wind rushed through Snug's fur and the wide world seemed to be swinging too, as the music of the mouth-organ sang below.

A shadow fell on the grass, the drum beat, the rabbit thumped its foot for DANGER, and the alarm trumpet sounded. Every animal fled to shelter, except little Snug who went on swinging.

'Stop! Stop!' cried the showman, taking cover, but it was too late. Down like a stone fell the hawk, down to the earth, for its eye had caught the gleam of Snug's red trousers. Then with Snug in its claws it rose in the air. It held Snug firmly by his trousers, and it carried him to the church tower where it had its nest.

All the young hawks were waiting for dinner.

They put their heads over the edge of the nest and watched their mother.

'There's something special today,' they told each other with shrill cries of hunger.

'Here's little Red Trousers for your dinner,' called the hawk, resting on the ledge of the tower.

'Please, please, please,' squeaked Snug.

'You are not very fat after all,' said the hawk, sternly, 'You are only a morsel among my family.'

The hawk fastened Snug to the iron weather-cock by his trousers and coat, and there he hung, swinging in the wind, while all the young birds cried for him.

Down flew the hawk, circling the valley, seeking more food.

Snug struggled but could not get free.

He dragged one arm from his jacket and then the other. Holding the metal foot of the weather-cock, he slipped his thin legs out of the trousers, which flapped in the wind. He hung by his tail for a moment, while his little coat and trousers ballooned on the weather-cock, just as if he were inside them.

He took one look at the earth far below, he gave a faint cry and then he dived into the air.

He landed, dazed and bruised, on a patch of moss, and he just managed to creep into the shelter of some ferns when the hawk returned.

'Quick! We are hungry!' screamed the little hawks, as the mother went to the weather-cock to seize the empty jacket and trousers.

'Gone! Vanished!' cried the astonished hawk.

Snug lay very still. After a time a ladybird found him and she gave him a spotted cloak to wrap round him. It was so small Snug used it as a handkerchief to dry his tears. A butterfly hovered near, and she gave him a sip of honey to revive him. Two ants brought an oak leaf to cover him. A sunbeam warmed him, and a spider spun a web over his cuts and hurts.

He lay there until it was dusk, when he ventured

out. He wandered a long way, lost in the wide countryside, until suddenly he saw the gleam of a tiny light. He crept up, and he tapped on a tiny door.

In the meantime Mr and Mrs Mouse and Serena were hunting everywhere.

The old showman hedgehog told how a hawk, a wind-hover, had carried off the little mouse.

'It was the red trousers, ma'am,' explained Pin Hedgehog. 'Too bright he was, like a poppy in a cornfield.'

Sadly they went home to the 'Rose and Crown'. At night Mrs Mouse put a lighted candle in her window, and Mr Mouse hung a lantern from the porch. He went out to ask all his friends to look for little Snug in field and dell.

'I'll go and hunt for him,' said Mr Toad, who was wandering in the lane.

Off he waddled and first he saw Policeman Owl sailing serenely over the hedge.

'Tawny! Tawny!' he called. 'Have you seen little Snug?'

'Too-whit, too-whoo,' hooted Tawny Owl. 'I saw a pair of red trousers on the weather-cock, but nobody was inside them.'

'Eaten up,' sighed the Toad. 'It's that hawk.' He asked moles, hedgehogs, bit-bats, snails, but nobody had seen little Snug. He trudged across the fields, and over the common. He was just going to turn back when he heard muffled laughter. He stopped. A small shrill voice was singing and he

recognized the song.

> 'Oh, the Rose and the Crown,
> With green leaves and brown,
> In summer and spring
> The turtle-doves sing,
> At the Rose and the Crown.
> It is fit for a King,
> Is the Rose and the Crown.'

'Where is he? Where is the varmint hiding?' cried Toad.

The laughter came from a bunch of straw in the tall wet grasses. A glow-worm light shone in a window.

'Is that you, Snug?' called Toad. The tiny door opened and a flood of light streamed out. Mr and Mrs Harvest and Snug looked down from the straw caravan.

'Oh, Mr Toad,' cried Snug, leaping down the step. 'Come inside. We're having supper.'

'Where have you been, Snug? Do you know your poor father is looking for you and your mother is weeping? Here you are, enjoying yourself. You ought to be ashamed!'

Toad was very indignant.

'Please sir,' interrupted Mr Harvest. 'Please, we found him lost and cold without his trousers and bruised with tumbling from the top of the church steeple. So we bandaged him and gave him a good feed and now he is singing to us.'

'Yes, Mr Toad,' said Snug, showing his bandages.

'Thank you very much,' cried Toad, shaking hands with the harvest mice. 'Thank you, and if you come to the "Rose and Crown", Mr William Mouse will thank you himself.'

The harvest mice said it had been a pleasure to entertain such a knowing little mouse as Snug.

'Now come along with me,' said Mr Toad, taking Snug's arm, and they crept slowly home.

What a greeting there was when they arrived! What drinks of hot milk with a sprig of lemon balm to keep out the cold!

'Oh, my darling Snug!' cried Mrs Mouse, throwing her arms round little Snug, so that he nearly choked. 'I am so glad to see you safe and sound! Never mind your old trousers. I will make a new pair tomorrow.'

'Not red trousers,' implored Snug. 'I don't want to be a poppy in the corn. I want to be invisible like the harvest mice.'

'Well, we'll see,' promised Mrs Mouse, smiling.

She bathed Snug's bruises in sweet balsam from her herb cupboard, and put on ointment of self-heal. The next day the little mouse was completely cured with never an ache or pain.

She stitched and stitched with her tiny needle and made a pair of brown trousers and a shadowy blue coat just like the smoke from a wood fire.

At night Snug skipped out to dance in the moonlight and Serena danced with him.

'Hello, Snug,' whispered the harvest mice, and Snug saw their straw caravan drawn up under a foxglove.

'Here we are,' said Mrs Harvest, shyly.

'Welcome! Welcome!' shouted Mr Mouse, as they walked into the house. 'Come and sit by my fire. Meet all my friends. Here's Mr Toad, and Samuel Furze and John Barleycorn, and Timothy, and my wife, all wishing to thank you.'

So they had supper, and the young ones sat on the floor for there wasn't room at the table. They sang merry songs, and toasted Mr and Mrs Harvest.

At last they all went to bed – the Toad in the guest room, the three old mice on the kitchen floor, and the harvest mice in the caravan. Snug begged to sleep there too, and he lay on a heap of straw, in the tiny yellow house.

The next day the caravan went away, filled with good food.

'We'll see you again, after the harvest,' called the little couple. 'Good-bye, Mr Mouse, and Mrs Mouse. Good-bye, Serena and Snug. Good-bye, Mr Toad.'

They trundled the caravan down the lane among the ferns and buttercups, and soon it was out of sight.

Snug and the Silver Spoon

One day Snug thought he would go a-fishing like his father.

'Please, Father, will you lend me your fishing-rod?' he asked.

'Certainly not,' answered Mr Mouse, who was busy boiling dandelions to make a yellow syrup. 'Come along, Snug! Make yourself useful! A fat little mouse like you ought to be able to stir my syrup.'

Snug took the long wooden spoon and stirred the mixture. Swirls of steam arose and he sniffed and sniffed. It was very nice!

'A pinch of ginger, and a piece of honeycomb, Snug,' said Mr Mouse, and he sprinkled the ginger and added the honey to the pan.

'And now, what did you say about fishing?' he asked.

'Please will you lend me your fishing-rod. I'm going a-fishing,' said Snug, boldly.

'Not with my rod, but you can make your own,' said Mr Mouse firmly. 'I'll show you while the dandelion syrup cools.'

He lifted the brass pan to the ground and then he
went out with Snug to the field.

'Get me some of those rushes,' said Mr Mouse.

Snug ran to gather the long green rushes. Mr
Mouse tied a wild strawberry to the tip for the bait.
He plaited the other end with bindweed to make a
handle.

'Now you can fish with this, and if you're lucky
you *may* catch a fish,' said he.

Little Serena came tumbling through the hedge,
eager to see what was happening.

'And what do you want, Miss Serena?' asked her
father.

'Please, a fishing-rod too. I want to go a-fishing,'
said Serena.

So Mr Mouse made another fishing-rod, and this time he tied a wild raspberry on the tip for the bait.

'Now you two can go a-fishing and don't you fall in. Take care of yourselves, and mind the Stoats and Weasels.'

'Yes, Father,' said Snug and Serena, obediently.

'And you'd better make a basket to carry home your catch. Make a big basket,' said Mr Mouse.

'Oh yes,' said Snug. 'I 'specks we shall catch a whale.'

Mr Mouse returned to the 'Rose and Crown' to finish his dandelion syrup, and the two little mice ran about gathering grasses to weave into a basket. They made a long-shaped basket, because fish are long, and they wove a cover to keep the fish from leaping out. So at last they went to the river.

Either the bait was too tasty, or the mice were not very clever, but every time they dipped the rods into the water a fish nibbled first at the strawberry, then at the raspberry.

62

'Very nice strawberries grow up there,' said one little fish to another. 'Snug and Serena are giving a party.'

'Nice raspberries too,' said the other fish.

'I wish something would happen,' said Serena, slowly, as she watched the ripples spreading in circles and the fish popping up their heads. 'I don't think I like fishing as much as I expected.'

A ripple spread across the water as a boat approached. The fishes hurried away, but Snug and Serena called as they recognized Mr Toad. His boat was a water-lily pad, and he rowed with a pair of slender oars.

He looked rather unhappy, and this was strange for Mr Toad was a calm and comfortable animal.

'It isn't on water and it isn't on land,' he murmured, staring at Snug and Serena as if he had forgotten them.

'Dear Mr Toad. Come and see us catching fish,' said Serena.

'It isn't in the mud and it isn't in the rushes,' said Mr Toad, miserably.

'What have you lost, Mr Toad?' asked Serena.

Then the Toad saw his friends.

'Snug and Serena! Oh dear me! I wonder if you can help,' said he. 'I've lost my silver spoon.'

'What is it like?' asked Snug.

'It is a very beautiful spoon, given to my ancestors. It has wavy lines like feathers round the handle, and it is small enough for a toad to use for his dinner. It was made by the royal silversmith for the little princess, but it was so tiny she gave it to a pet toad. He lived in her garden, and he ate from a little bowl of food she prepared for him every day. So she gave him this tiny silver spoon. To her surprise he took it in his hand and lapped up his soup. The king and the courtiers came to see the marvel, but this frightened the toad so much he waddled away with the spoon and never returned.'

'Oh, Mr Toad,' murmured Serena. 'Oh!'

'He was my great-great-great-grandfather, Sir Timothy Toad,' continued Mr Toad. 'Now I have lost my spoon. I am downhearted.'

Two round tears fell from the Toad's eyes and rolled across the lily-pad into the river.

'Poor Mr Toad,' said Serena. 'We will help you to look.'

'Where did you lose it?' asked the practical Snug.

'Nowhere! It disappeared from my castle. It vanished. It faded away. One day it lay in the glass case, and the next day it had gone. Nobody came in. It went. Clean gone,' said he.

'Clean gone,' echoed Snug.

Mr Toad paddled away and the two mice filled the empty basket with flowers and went home.

'What, no fish?' cried Mr Mouse, looking at the flowers.

'Never a one,' sighed Serena. 'And Mr Toad has

lost his silver spoon.'

'That magical spoon?' cried Mrs Mouse, holding up her paws in horror. 'It's a wonderful spoon.'

'Yes,' added Mr Mouse. 'If you stir your broth with it you can get any taste you like. Egg broth, chicken broth, nettle soup, dandelion soup. It doesn't matter.'

'I've heard that if you eat with that little silver spoon, you can have anything you fancy,' said Mrs Mouse. 'Cheese or bacon rinds or—'

'Wild strawberries and cream?' asked Serena.

'Anything. Anything you fancy,' said Mr Mouse.

Mrs Mouse began to sweep her clean little house. She hunted among Toad's bedclothes in the best bedroom. Mr Mouse searched the cellars. There was no sign of the silver spoon.

'How many fishes did you catch?' asked John Barleycorn.

66

'None,' answered Snug. 'They ate our bait.'

'Ne'er a one,' grumbled Samuel Furze. 'I wanted a sprat for my supper and you can't even catch a minnow.'

'Perhaps I shall catch a silver spoon,' said Snug hopefully.

Mrs Mouse was tired. She packed the children off to bed, and sent the three old talkative mice home.

'Good night, good night, good night,' they called, and they wandered away peeping in the ferns and leaves for the silver spoon. The moon shone down making everything silver.

The next morning Snug and Serena set off to

hunt. They turned over the pebbles and out ran creepy-crawly creatures.

'Have you seen a silver spoon?' asked Serena.

'No, sir! Please, sir! No, sir!' said the ant, Mrs Emmet. They asked the cockchafer, Jim Bassett, but he had not seen the spoon in his flight. Miss Hodmadod the snail, who sat at the door of her striped shell, said she had a silver spoon of her own so small nobody could see it.

> 'Silver spoon,
> Silver spoon.
> All things are silver,
> Under the moon,'

she sang in her wavering tiny treble.

Snug met Mr and Mrs Harvest with their caravan and baskets. They were on their way to the Fair.

'Mr Harvest,' called Snug. 'Have you got a silver spoon?'

'Can't say that I have, Snug,' said Mr Harvest. 'I've got a wooden spoon.'

'No,' added Mrs Harvest, 'but once we found one, left behind after a picnic. Oh my! It was heavy! We carried it in our caravan, and we left it at the door of the farmhouse, for a present for the new-born babby. It's lucky to have a silver spoon. They were pleased, but of course they thought it was from a fairy, and it was from us, me and him.'

'This is a silver spoon belonging to Mr Toad,' explained Serena. 'It is a very little spoon, but it is magical.'

'Ah! Then it must have been took by yon fairies, as dances by night,' said Mr Harvest.

Poor Mr Toad wandered up and down. He got quite thin and his clothes hung from his shoulders like a scarecrow's.

Mrs Dumble, his housekeeper, was worried. 'There now, Mr Toad! Don't ye take on so. It will turn up. Come and have a nice cup of tea, sir.'

'Who can have taken it?' said Mr Toad for the hundredth time.

'Who indeed? The varmint!' said Mrs Dumble.

'It isn't the Stoat or the Owl or the Weasel. It isn't the grasshopper or ladybird,' said Toad.

He peered closely at the glass case, and he saw a

small mark, a scratch on the wall and a dampish patch below.

'Somebody has been here again,' said he. 'I know this mark. It's the baby Otter. There's a baby in the river for I've seen him playing with his mother. He's taken my silver spoon. I shall never get it back now. I can tackle a weasel or a stoat on occasions, but not an otter.'

'Hotters are too big. Playful a baby Hotter may be, but too big,' said Mrs Dumble, mournfully.

It was quite true. The baby Otter had stretched his sleek arm through the window and seized the bright silver spoon. He tossed it up and caught it. He licked it and he bit it. Then after a game of catch he tired of the little flashing thing. He dropped it on a lily-pad and left it, then he dived in the river to try to catch a fish.

The little fishes found the spoon on the lily. They grabbed it with their soft lips and swam with it. They

strove to take it from one another. They played tug-of-war with it. At last they, too, tired of it, and down fell the silver spoon to a rock.

When Snug and Serena were told by Mr Toad that a baby Otter had taken the spoon, they knelt on the river bank and tried to see the Otter. They saw the wet round head and the bright eyes and the sleek arms of the baby Otter as it plunged and dived.

'Oh, Otter! Otter! Have you seen a silver spoon?' sang Serena in her sweetest voice.

'Is that a mermaid singing?' asked the Otter looking round.

'It's only me, Serena. Have you seen a silver spoon?' sang Serena in her high little voice.

'Silver spoon? Yes, I left it on a lily-pad, and now it's gone,' said the Otter and he dived away.

'Let's make two new fishing-rods and fish for it,' said Snug.

So they picked some rushes and bound the handles of the rods with bindweed, and put little buns for bait from their mother's baking.

As before, the fish came whisking up and gobbled the bait in a minute.

'Oh, little fish,' called Serena. 'We don't want to catch you. We are after a silver spoon.'

'I've seen that spoon,' answered a fish. 'It's down on a rock. What will you give me if I bring it to you?'

'A pot of our mother's strawberry jam,' said Serena.

'No, our mother makes lily jam, thank you,' replied the fish.

'Cowslip wine and primrose syrup,' said Snug.

'No, we have enough wine in the river,' said the fish.

'I'll give you a little ship made out of a walnut shell, which was in my stocking at Christmas,' said Snug.

'Yes,' shouted all the fish together in silvery voices. 'Yes, a walnut-shell boat.'

So away ran Snug and Serena to their home. They fetched the walnut ship with its silk sails from Snug's bedroom. It was a treasure, but they knew they would give anything to help Mr Toad, their friend.

When they returned, the silver spoon lay on a water-lily, and all the little fishes poked their faces up to watch.

'Can't swim to it,' said Snug.

The fish then came to the bank, carrying the spoon, and Snug leaned over and took it. He floated the walnut ship on the water.

'Thank you, oh, thank you,' shrilled the little fish, and Snug and Serena danced their way home with the spoon in the fishing-basket.

There was no need to go all the way to Mr Toad's Castle. The old Toad sat in the porch of the 'Rose and Crown', talking to the three ancient mice. They could hear him down the garden.

'Yes, it was a magical spoon, made of pure silver, given to my ancestor by the princess.'

'A great loss,' moaned John and Samuel and Timothy.

Then down the path came Snug and Serena, carrying the basket.

'We've caught a silver fish,' they laughed to Mr Toad.

'Ah,' cried Mr Toad, rushing to them. 'What do I see? My silver spoon? Where did it come from?'

He nearly wept as he clasped the little spoon to his heart.

'From the river. The fishes gave it to us,' said Snug. He did not tell the Toad they had exchanged their treasure for it.

'Now do some magic with it,' implored Serena.

Mr Toad stroked his spoon and Snug went for a glass of the dandelion brew. Mr Toad stirred it with his spoon, and they all had a taste. It was like cowslips and roses and oranges and strawberries all mixed in one delicious drink.

'Oh, 'larcious,' exclaimed Snug.

'Beautiful,' sighed Serena, but the three old mice finished it up at once.

'Another magic,' begged Serena.

Mr Toad dropped some dandelion seeds in the silver spoon, and blew them. They floated off like silk parachutes with butterflies flying near them.

'Now I will give a reward to the little fishes who

found my spoon,' said Mr Toad.

He went to the river with Serena and Snug. He played a tune on his fiddle to summon the fish. Then he held up the spoon.

'The blessings of the wind and the sun, the moon and the earth be upon you,' said he. 'May nobody ever fish with rod or line or net in this part of the river. May you be free.'

And the strange thing was, that nobody, man or animal, could ever fish in that stretch of water again.

The Mouse Telegrams

Little fieldmice have four birthdays a year. It is a special gift from Mother Nature to make up for their small size. So Serena Mouse had a spring birthday, a summer birthday, an autumn and a winter one. Spring was a yellow birthday, summer a blue one, autumn was brown and winter snow-white.

It was Serena's spring birthday, and even Mrs Mouse had forgotten, but the cuckoo reminded her.

'Cuckoo! Cuckoo! Birthday! Birthday!' sang the bird as soon as it arrived from over the sea, and Mrs Mouse looked up from her ironing.

'Goodness me! I quite forgot little Serena!' she cried. 'Serena! Serena!' she called. 'It's your birthday, your spring birthday.'

Serena ran in from the garden, followed by Snug.

'Can we have a party?' she asked.

76

'Yes,' said Mrs Mouse, and she went back to her ironing.

'Oh thank you! A birthday party, and yellow presents,' cried the little mice dancing round their mother.

'Now do be quiet! You'll make me burn your father's shirts. I must think about this party,' said Mrs Mouse.

'Can we invite Mr Toad?' asked Serena.

'And Mr and Mrs Harvest?' added Snug.

'And little Dan Dormouse? He is my particular friend,' said Serena.

'And the gypsy hedgehogs?' asked Snug.

'Yes. They can all come if they want,' said Mrs Mouse.

'Shall we write letters to invite them?' asked Serena.

'It's too late for the post. Robin Redbreast has flown away,' said Mrs Mouse, looking rather worried.

'Shall we be postmen?' asked Snug.

'No, that is impossible,' said Mrs Mouse sadly. 'Mr Toad lives far off down by the river. The gypsy hedgehogs will be wandering with their tent and cooking-pot, visiting a Fair, playing their mouth-organ. No use trying to find them.'

'And Mr and Mrs Harvest will be making baskets in their caravan. We can't find the harvest mice,' added Serena. 'Dan Dormouse will be in the woods and we shall *never* discover him.'

'Hush,' cried Mrs Mouse, putting her iron back on the fire. 'Stay quiet and let me think, for this is a puzzle.'

The little mice stayed very still listening to the thoughts of everything. The clock was ticking and that was the clock's thinking. The fire was crackling and that was the fire thinking. The brook was burbling and that was the water thinking.

'Everybody's thinking,' whispered Serena.

''cept me,' whispered Snug.

'Well, I've had my think,' said Mrs Mouse in a soft mysterious voice. 'We will send a mouse-telegram.'

'Oh! Oh!' murmured the two mice, opening wide their eyes. 'What is a mouse-telegram, Mother?'

'It's an ancient quick way of sending a message,' said Mrs Mouse. 'It's a magical way, known only to animals.'

'Yes,' whispered the mice. 'Nobody but us.'

'You must pick a red-tipped daisy, and there's magic in that,' said Mrs Mouse.

'Yes,' breathed the little brown mice.

'And a double celandine, and there's a wish in that.'

'Yes,' said the mice. 'Yes, Mother.'

'And an oxlip, and there's a wish in that.'

'Yes, Mother,' said the little mice.

'And a white violet. Bring them all to me and I'll send the telegram,' said Mrs Mouse.

Off ran little Snug and Serena into the fields, peeping under leaves, peering at the petals of flowers, for magical flowers are not easy to find. In a daisy-field Serena discovered a daisy with red frilly petals. Then Snug found a double celandine growing in a wet ditch.

They ran to a cowslip field, for among cowslips there is often an oxlip, and every country child knows that a wish goes with an oxlip.

Lastly they hunted under the hedges for the first white violet.

'Here they are, Mother. Here are the telegram flowers,' called the mice as they scampered up the garden to the 'Rose and Crown'.

Mrs Mouse tossed the blossoms up in the air for the wind to catch. As the strong South wind carried them away she called, 'Telegrams! Telegrams! Mr Toad, Mr and Mrs Harvest, Mr and Mrs Hedgehog, little Dan Dormouse. You are invited to Serena's party.'

Mr Toad got his telegram as he sat on a lily-leaf fishing in the river. 'Serena's spring birthday,' said he, and he wound up his line and shut his fishing basket. He paddled across to Toad's Castle and fetched a sack from the cellar. Then he gave a whistle and a flock of yellow butterflies flew down and entered the sack.

'Serena will like these butterflies,' said he to his housekeeper, Mrs Dumble. 'I'm off to her birthday party. Just had a telegram.'

'Take these cheesecakes,' cried Mrs Dumble, running to the larder and returning with a basket of yellow cakes.

So Mr Toad set off at his slow amble for the 'Rose and Crown'.

Mr and Mrs Harvest were busy making baskets far away on the common when down fluttered an oxlip.

'Where has this come from?' asked Mrs Harvest, but Mr Harvest sniffed the sweet scent and knew it was a telegram.

'It's Serena's spring birthday,' said he, 'and us is asked to the party. That's a treat!'

They dabbled their paws in the stream and brushed their clothes.

'Us'll take her a rush basket with a yellow corn-cake inside, and a necklace of wheat ears,' said Mrs Harvest.

They packed the basket and set off for the 'Rose and Crown'.

Mr and Mrs Hedgehog were at the village fair when a white violet fell on them from the sky.

'What does this mean, wife?' asked Mr Hedgehog.

'A white violet means good luck,' said Mrs Hedgehog.

'It means more than that,' said Mr Hedgehog. 'It's a mouse-telegram, asking us to Serena's party.'

'Then we can't go,' said Mrs Hedgehog, firmly. 'We can't leave the fairground. We are too busy.'

They went back to the swings and roundabouts, calling, 'Two a penny. Take your seats,' while little animals paid their pence and swung to the music of Mr Hedgehog's mouth-organ.

Little Dan Dormouse was rolling through the leafy tunnels of a hedge when a double celandine fell on his back.

He ran home to show his mother the frill of petals.
'That's a telegram,' said Mrs Dormouse.
'What's a telegram?' asked Dan.
'A double-quick message. It is sent on double petals to get here quickly. It's an invitation to Serena's party.'

Mrs Dormouse started off to find a present. A furze bush grew like a golden fire in the hedge, and she picked some of the pea-shaped flowers. She pressed them together and she made a yellow muff just right for Serena's paws.

'Now take this present, and go carefully, with your eyes wide open for dangers,' said Mrs Dormouse as she kissed her small furry son.

Somebody else got a telegram. Snug sent a secret telegram, as he tossed a dandelion up in the air.

'Dandy-Lion, come to the party,' he sang. Then he whispered, 'I only want to know if it works.'

The wind carried off the flower, and away danced Snug.

Mr Stoat lay in his underground room, dozing with his head on a lumpy pillow. A dandelion came floating down the chimney.

'Hello,' said he, as he sniffed the strong smell. 'What's this? A telegram? An invitation to Serena's party? It must be a mistake but I'll go. I'm a Dandy-Lion.'

He brushed his tawny coat and pointed his whiskers. Then he skipped up and down looking for a present.

'Ha! A mousetrap!' he muttered. 'Just right.'

At the 'Rose and Crown' everybody was very busy, cooking, baking, setting the table and preparing for Serena's party.

There were curdy cakes and lemon cheese tarts, orange slices and lemon buns. There was primrose

wine, and cowslips in sugar, marigold buds in nectar, with buttercup ices and dried mallow cheeses. In the centre of the table was the birthday cake with lots of little candles on top, one for every happy day.

Snug walked slowly round, counting the plates. Then he put another for his dandelion guest.

He shivered as he peeped through the window. He nearly leapt out of his skin when he saw something glide round the garden like a golden lion. It stooped under the lavender bush and put a shiny present there.

'Oh dear! The S-s-s-,' stammered Snug. 'Oh dear! The Dandy-dandy-dandy! The Lion! The Lion!'

'Whatever is the matter?' asked Mrs Mouse.

'Nothing,' muttered Snug. 'It's a Dandy-dande-lion out there, wanting to come in.'

'Nonsense,' said Mrs Mouse, and she looked out. 'There's nothing and nobody.'

It was true. All was quiet and the shining streak of dandelion had gone.

'There's Mr and Mrs Harvest,' called Serena, and the two harvest mice dragged their caravan to the door.

'Come in, Mr and Mrs Harvest,' said Mrs Mouse, and Mr Mouse ran up from the cellar to welcome them.

'Us wishes Serena many happy returns of the day,' said Mrs Harvest, bobbing a curtsey.

'Yes, us wishes that,' added Mr Harvest, bowing.

'Us made her a basket,' continued Mrs Harvest.

'And here her be,' added Mr Harvest, bringing the tiny rush basket from behind his back and giving it to Serena.

Mr Mouse offered the harvest mice a drink of honey wine in an acorn cup and the two sat admiring the laden table.

'Did you see a Dandy-Lion?' asked Snug.

'Lots and lots,' said Mrs Harvest, and Mr Harvest added, 'Lots and lots and lots.'

Then came a shout and a halloo, and little Dan Dormouse rolled in at the door like a furry ball. He was so entangled it took Mrs Mouse some time to set him free.

The old fieldmice came hobbling after him, waving their sticks and shouting to Mr Mouse and Serena.

'Happy birthday, everybody,' they cried.

'We've brought Serena some presents,' said Samuel Furze.

They all fumbled in their pockets and each brought out of the green depths of his trousers a tiny doll made of the white pith of rushes.

'They'll go yaller in time,' said Timothy Snout.

'How lovely,' cried Serena. 'I've never had a dolly. Thank you, dear Mr Mouses.'

The three old mice sat down at the table and began to eat.

All this time Snug had been peering from the window, but there was no sign of the strange guest.

'Did you see a Dandy-Lion?' he asked.

'Many a one,' said the three mice, helping themselves to the food.

'There's Mr Toad,' cried Serena, running down the path to meet the stout animal.

'Happy birthday, my dear,' said Mr Toad, and he untied the sack. Out flew the cloud of brimstone butterflies, dancing in a circle round Serena's head.

She clapped her paws in delight, and when Mr Toad went indoors she stayed in the garden, watching the pretty flock. They fluttered across the grass and entered a little wire house which lay under the lavender bush. They sipped the piece of honeycomb which lay inside.

'What is this?' cried Serena. 'A house for me!'

She ran inside singing:

> 'Just the house for me!
> Just the house for me!
> A little wee house,
> Just right for a mouse,
> And honeycomb for tea!'

There was a snap! The door shut, and she was caught in the mousetrap.

Out from the bushes came the Stoat, and away flew the butterflies in a fright. The Stoat picked up the

little mousetrap, with Serena inside and rushed off with it under his arm.

'Mother! Mother! Mr Toad! Oh! Oh!' cried Serena.

'Don't be frightened,' said the Stoat. 'You are safe with me.'

'I want to go home to my party,' sobbed Serena, running up and down and beating her small fists against the wires. 'Let me go, naughty Stoat.'

The Stoat dashed on. He ran down the passage and put the mousetrap on the floor of his house.

'Now Serena, here you will live, and you may as well stop crying for you can't escape,' said he. 'I always wanted a nice little fieldmouse to sing to me. Sing that song about the house.'

'I can't,' sobbed Serena. 'Let me go or Mr Toad will come after you and my father will bring a big stick and beat you, and Snug will bite you.'

'Why, it was Snug who invited me to your party,' said the Stoat. 'He sent a mouse-telegram of a Dandy-Lion to me.'

Serena was so startled she said no more. She crouched in a corner of the trap and wept little tears that rolled out like pearls.

'I can't abide a weeping mouse,' said the Stoat, crossly. 'I'm going out, and mind your tears are dried when I come back. I don't like a wet floor!'

He leapt over the heap of bones, shut the door and locked it after him, and away he went.

Serena tried to raise the catch of the mousetrap, but she was too feeble. She called, but the Stoat's house was underground, and nobody could hear her little squeaks.

There was a flutter in the chimney and down to the ugly room came the flock of golden butterflies, like sunshine and primroses floating there.

'Oh save me! Save me!' cried Serena, and the butterflies darted around her and then flew back up the chimney. Soon they returned with a long green thread of plaited grasses, which they tied in a butterfly bow to the side of the mousetrap.

The butterflies pulled in a dancing, wavering crowd, but the trap did not move.

'Of course you can't help me,' sighed Serena. 'You are not strong enough.'

Up the chimney they flew again with the end of the thread, out into the wood. Mr Toad waited there,

near the chimney, among the grasses he had plaited
so neatly. He wrapped the end of the thread round
his own stout body and then he pulled, slowly walking
away. The mousetrap jerked and bumped across the
bony floor of the Stoat's house, and up the chimney
with little Serena rattling like a pea inside it. Up to
the woodland it came, and Mr Toad unfastened the
door. Little Serena escaped from her prison.

'Oh, Mr Toad! You have saved me, you and all
the yellow butterflies!' she cried, embracing the fat

old Toad, while the brimstones danced in the air
around her head.

'Quick! Quick! No time to lose,' murmured Mr
Toad, and he took her trembling hand and hurried

her away.

'How did you know where I was?' she panted.

'I followed the butterflies,' said Mr Toad.

'I came as fast as I could toddle, for I knew where Mr Stoat lives. I couldn't get down the chimney, of course, so I sent a rope by the butterflies when Mr Stoat left the house.'

'Serena! Where have you been?' asked Mrs Mouse.

'She was took,' said the Toad, pointing a finger at Snug. 'She was took by a Dandy-Lion!'

Snug hung his head. 'I'm sorry, Serena. I never knew. I never thought.'

Serena was so glad to get home she could not speak. She sat down at the table and drank ten cups of tea and ate a candle, she was so hungry. The old mice had finished off everything except the candles on the cake.

'Where did you go?' whispered Snug.

'I'll tell you later,' murmured Serena, taking up another yellow candle and nibbling it.

So when all the guests had gone home, and the tea-things were washed up, Serena told her story. Mr Toad stayed behind to hear and he nodded his head as she talked.

'Mouse-telegrams are dangerous things,' said he. 'You never know if the right people will get them.'